I0536664

Live Free or Tri

A collection of three short mystery stories

By Judy Penz Sheluk

Copyright @ January 2016 Judy Penz Sheluk

www.judypenzsheluk.com

All rights reserved. No part of this book shall be used or reproduced in any manner whatsoever without written permission, except in the case of brief quotations embodied in critical articles and reviews. The scanning, uploading and distribution of this book via the Internet, or via any other means, without the permission of the author, is illegal and punishable by law. Please purchase only authorized electronic editions and do not participate or encourage electronic piracy of copyrighted materials. Your support of authors' rights is appreciated.

Proofread by Jennifer Grybowski

Formatting by intentionmedia

This is a work of fiction. Names, characters, places, and events described herein are the product of the author's imagination or are used fictitiously. Any similarity to actual events, locations, organizations, or persons, living or dead, is entirely coincidental and not intended by the author.

Paperback: 978-0-9950007-1-1

ISBN eBook: 978-0-9950007-0-4

Author's Note: *Live Free or Die* is included in WORLD ENOUGH AND CRIME, a crime fiction anthology edited by Donna & Alex Carrick (October 2014, Carrick Publishing)

For Jenn and Michelle: thanks for everything

TABLE OF CONTENTS

Live Free or Tri
A collection of three short mystery stories

By Judy Penz Sheluk
For Jenn: beta reader, proofreader, friend

LIVE FREE OR DIE

The first time any of us met Jack he was wearing a dark green suit. That seemed odd to me. It wasn't St. Patrick's Day, and the office attire was mostly business casual, with an emphasis on the casual. This was especially true in "cubicle hell," where an overworked staff of four plus supervisor made collection calls and routinely canceled insurance policies for non-payment.

Later, Jack would confide in me that the green suit was his only suit. "Wear a green suit and everyone assumes you must own a black one, a brown one, and a blue one," he had said, and I had to admit it made sense. But the first time I met him, my only thought was, "Green suit, can't be from around here."

I should have known Jack was going to be trouble right from the beginning. In my defense I was twenty-one to his thirty-one, and until a few months before, when I'd been dumped for a girl with the improbable name of Ankh, I'd had the same boyfriend throughout high school.

Anyway, my inexperience with men aside, there was something riveting about Jack. It was more than his stature—six-feet-two with the build of an athlete; you could imagine six-pack abs and muscled thighs—more than the penetrating stare of eyes a bluish shade of tanzanite verging on violet. It was as if he wore his charisma like a suit of armor and polished it up every morning.

Jack came to the company as an efficiency expert, imported from the U.S. Head Office in Portsmouth, New Hampshire, to the Canadian head office in Toronto. The suburb of Don Mills to be exact.

Apparently we were inefficient at collecting monies owed. I could have told them it was because we tended to empathize with the insured, if only because we were all stone broke ourselves. Thanks to our minimum wage jobs and age-rated auto insurance, most of us couldn't afford to pay the premiums, let alone own a car. Extending payment terms for a week or two, where was the harm in that?

My first mistake was agreeing to have lunch with Jack, though to be fair, he asked all five of us in the Credit Department, each on a separate day. My day of the week was Friday. Jack made me feel as though he'd saved the best for last.

He drove a midnight blue Chevy pick-up with a front bench seat and extended cab. The license plate included the message, "LIVE FREE OR DIE," which Jack informed me was the State motto of New Hampshire. I preferred Ontario's more mundane "YOURS TO DISCOVER," but I'll admit to being somewhat biased.

I suppose I was expecting a sandwich at the local deli, or maybe fish and chips from Captain Sam's, given it was Friday. Both were just south of the office, and regular hangouts for the many white-collar workers in the area. But Jack drove west on Eglinton. Clearly we were going to take more than my allotted hour for lunch.

"Molly tells me you like authentic Mexican," Jack said, not taking his eyes off the road. "I was in Toronto a few years back. I remember a decent place on Yonge Street. Viva something-or-the-other."

Molly was my supervisor. I wondered how the subject of my food preferences had come up. "Molly told you that I like Mexican food?"

Jack grinned, his teeth flashing in the sunlight. "Let's just say I was curious about you."

The Mexican restaurant was no longer in business, but that didn't stop Jack. He navigated the truck into a tight parking spot along the street, hopped out, put change in the meter, opened my door, and led me to a British-style pub a couple of blocks down.

"It's not Mexican, but I was here a couple of nights ago," he said. "Typical pub food, but a good atmosphere, and a nice selection of draft beer."

I don't like beer, but the idea of dining out in a pub on a workday lunch hour had a certain charm. "I could go for an order of bangers and mash," I said, trying to demonstrate my worldly knowledge of tavern fare.

"So could I," Jack said, and chuckled softly. I got the distinct impression we weren't talking about the same thing, and found that I didn't necessarily mind. It had been a long time since Norbert had dumped me.

Lunch lasted a couple of hours, during which time I found myself telling Jack my life story, or at least the *Reader's Digest* version. I even told him my real name was Emerald, although everyone called me Emmy. It was only after we were headed back to the office that I realized he hadn't shared anything about himself.

"How long are you going to be in Toronto?" I asked.

"For a while. I'm starting with the Credit Department, but there are inefficiencies in all areas of the company that need to be identified and resolved."

"So you're moving here?"

Jack nodded. "I have a one-year contract. The company found me a rental apartment near Fairview Mall. But I'll be doing surprise audits in other cities now and again. I'll also be going home to New Hampshire for a few days every three weeks or so. To be honest, I'm already homesick. It's lonely, not knowing anyone."

"You've met a few people in the office, though, haven't you? I mean, besides those of us in Credit?"

"Oh sure, but it's not like anyone's really opened up to me. Not the way you did, Emerald."

"Emmy," I said, embarrassed. "And you're just being kind. I probably bored you to tears."

"Not at all. As a matter of fact, I'd like to get to know you quite a bit better."

And that's the way it started. We spent every moment of the weekend together, walking downtown for hours, taking in the CN Tower, the Eaton's Centre, Yorkville, Yonge Street, City Hall, old and new. We made plans to visit the Royal Ontario Museum, the Art Gallery of Ontario—even the Bata Shoe Museum. Jack's thirst to see and experience everything was contagious, and I found myself being a tourist in my own hometown, and loving every minute of it.

We were driving back to his place late Saturday night when he mentioned that it might be best if we keep our friendship a secret. "Not that we have anything to hide," he said, "but why fan the flames?" I thought about my co-workers, gossips each and every one of them, and my supervisor, Molly, who didn't appear to care much for Jack—likely because she felt her job was in jeopardy—and decided he was probably right.

"Okay." I edged myself closer to the passenger door, not quite sure what else to say.

"Why don't you slide over here, Emmy," Jack said, patting the seat beside him. "Otherwise, folks might think we're married."

**

It was about six weeks later when Molly came to my desk, carrying a card and a large brown envelope. Jack was back home in New Hampshire for a few days, returning midweek. I missed him.

"I'm collecting for the Jack and Jill shower on Wednesday," she said, handing me the card and the envelope. "Whatever you can afford."

I looked at the card, which had an image of a man and woman holding hands and standing under a white umbrella, a glittery rainbow behind them. It was the first I'd heard about a Jack and Jill shower, but then again, I'd kept pretty much to myself since getting involved with Jack. It was safer that way.

"Who's getting married?"

Molly gave me an odd look. "Well, Jack, of course, and what's totally ironic is that his fiancée's name is actually Jill. I thought he would have told you that day at lunch. You were gone long enough. Say you weren't ... "

"Of course not," I said, fighting the urge to throw up.

"It's just that Jack developed a bit of a reputation as a womanizer the last time he was here. Of course, that was five years ago. He could have changed."

It was the way she said it, more than what she said, that made me realize why Molly didn't care for Jack. And it had nothing whatsoever to do with job security.

Five years ago, Molly had been me.

**

"He slept with you, didn't he?" Jill spoke so quietly I almost convinced myself she didn't say it. I took a deviled egg from the paper plate on my lap and popped half of it in my mouth, trying to look nonchalant.

"Didn't he?" Jill said, again. Her otherwise pale cheeks had bright red splotches on them, as if someone had decided to paint a clown's face on her.

Jack was standing at the other side of the room, his back to us. He was laughing at something one of the sales guys had said. He hadn't said one word to me since he'd gotten back. Hadn't given me so much as a passing glance.

"I didn't know about you, Jill. You have to believe me. I'm not the kind ... I know what it feels like ... "

Jill looked over at Jack, who was still kibitzing with the sales team, then back at me. "We need to talk. Somewhere private. Tonight, when Jack's out drinking with his buddies."

I agreed to meet her for dinner at a local Italian restaurant known for its great food, good wine, and generously proportioned booths—an entirely sensible combination of public and private. After all, I had no idea what Jill wanted to discuss with me, but I was pretty sure she wasn't going to ask me to be in the wedding party.

**

"Let me start by saying that I believe you, Emmy," Jill said.

We were sitting near the back of the Italian restaurant—our choice given it was a Wednesday night and there was plenty of available seating. We'd ordered a liter of house red and a basket of bruschetta to split as an appetizer. The whole thing felt a bit surreal.

"I appreciate that you're taking my word for it," I said, fingering a piece of bruschetta. I didn't have the appetite to bite into it.

"It's not like you were the first. And you're unlikely to be the last." Jill studied the diamond ring on her left hand. "I suppose I thought once we were engaged Jack would stop misbehaving."

"How long have you been engaged?"

"Three months. About a month longer than you've been sleeping with him, if my math is correct."

It was. "You're still willing to marry him?"

"I suppose you think that's pathetic."

I thought about my initial reaction when I found out about Norbert and Ankh. Devastation, certainly, but also a sense of determination, an irrational desire to win Norbert back, if only to be the dumper versus the dumpee. "I understand what it's like to invest years in a person. You don't want to think it was all a big waste of time."

Jill nodded. "That's exactly how I felt before we got engaged. But now I'm done. Finished. You were the last straw. No offense."

"None taken."

"Good. Now, the way I figure it, Jack owes both of us, and more than just an apology. What I'm wondering is, how would you like to get even?"

"Get even with Jack?"

Jill nodded again. "You see I have a plan and I need your help to pull it off."

＊＊

There are times when you have to commit a crime to prevent an even bigger one. At least, that's what I tell myself when I can't sleep at night.

I'm not going to go into a lot of detail here. Suffice it to say that if we had implemented Jill's original plan we both could have done twenty-five to life. What did either of us know about guns? As much as I hated Jack in the moment, as much as I commiserated with Jill, I wasn't about to go to prison for either one of them.

Which is exactly why I came up with my own plan.

I never said it was perfect.

**

"Live free or die." Jill and I spoke the rehearsed lines in perfect unison when Jack walked through the door. We were standing in Jack's apartment, and by the shocked look on his face, he wasn't expecting to find his fiancée and mistress waiting for him.

"What are you two talking about?"

"Live free," I began.

"Or die," Jill finished.

"Free of the cushy job that allows you to travel across North America and pick up unsuspecting women," I said. "Women who don't know that you're already spoken for."

"Free of all your money—well, actually, free of anything you own of value," Jill said. "I just wish the pick-up truck was black. I've never been a fan of midnight blue."

"You can always trade it in, Jill, maybe get a nice little sports car," I said. "A black one."

"I'm not sure I'm following," Jack said, but it was clear from the hint of perspiration forming on his forehead and upper lip that he was getting the gist of it.

"It's actually very simple," I said. "Tomorrow morning, you're going to hand in your resignation, citing personal reasons. Then you're going to go back to New Hampshire on your own dime."

"Except you won't have a dime—or a vehicle, come to that," Jill added. "Because you're going to transfer all of your money into my personal bank account. And your vehicle ownership into my name. Don't worry, we'll come with you so you don't screw it up."

"What you're asking is preposterous," Jack said, his face flushed. "Why would I do any of that?"

"Because if you don't, I'll have to tell upper management how you took advantage of your position of authority and how you coerced me into bed." I leaned back into the wall. "Perhaps I'll even hire a lawyer, file a sexual harassment suit. The company would love that."

"Maybe I wasn't completely upfront with you," Jack said, "but there was no coercion." He turned to face Jill. "As for the money and the truck, you're delusional if you think I'm just going to hand it over."

"It's called payback time, Jack, for being a liar and a cheat." Jill folded her arms in front of her. "Consider it a pre-nup, without the nuptials."

"Of course, you're perfectly free to ignore the 'live free' part of this plan," I said.

That got Jack's interest. "What happens if I decide to do that? Ignore the 'live free' part?"

"Ah," Jill said. "That's where the 'or die' part comes in."

Jack had the nerve to laugh, the smug S.O.B. "You two? You're threatening to kill me? Just how do you propose to do that?"

"Let's just say that you'd never see it coming," Jill said.

I nodded and tried to look menacing.

I'm not sure Jack believed us, but in the end he chose to live free. Who wouldn't, given the option? After all, living free had its benefits—at least you were living without the threat of death hovering like a dark shadow.

There were some negotiations, of course. I like to think we were reasonable in our demands, and the reality is that despite his philandering ways, Jill still wanted to marry Jack. Especially since she'd found out she was pregnant. I didn't pretend to understand—surely she and the baby would be better off without him—but it wasn't my place to judge.

We eventually agreed that Jack could keep his job. That Jill would move into his apartment. They'd get married earlier than planned, given Jill was now with child. And that way we could both keep an eye on him, me at work, her at home. Ultimately, it would mean more money for Jill and the baby, since his paycheck was going to be directly deposited into her personal bank account. All Jack had to do was stay on the straight and narrow.

Some men never learn.

**

"Seriously," Molly said. "A green suit? At a funeral?"

I didn't tell her it was Jack's only suit. Maybe when they'd dated five years ago, he had other suits. Suits no longer in style, or maybe too big or too small. Maybe he'd lied to me and had a closetful, ready to pull out for a special occasion. It hardly mattered any longer.

"I don't mind the green," I said, more for something to say than anything else.

We both stared at the open casket, at Jack's hands clasped loosely together in front of his stomach. The mortician had done a good job of disguising the damage from the accident. I could have said Jack looked at peace, but I didn't believe it.

"A true tragedy," Molly said. "Jack falling into the subway tracks like that." She gave me an odd look, eyebrows raised, lips pursed. "Do you . . . do you think he'd been drinking?"

"I don't know." And I didn't. All I knew was that the ruling of accidental death would haunt me forever.

Jill was sitting in a pew at the side of the chapel, a black lace shawl draped loosely around her shoulders, her face bent down in prayer. For a moment, I thought she glanced my way, but I couldn't be certain. The next time I looked, her eyes were averted, a solitary teardrop finding its way down her face.

MURDER IN THE MARSH

Carrie Anne Camack pulled into the parking lot of the Asnorveldt Public Library. There were only six spaces, but she wasn't worried about finding a spot. The sun was just starting to rise, and besides, the library was closed on Sundays. Even if it was open, it was unlikely that all the spots would be taken; only the residents of the surrounding Holland Marsh could possibly find their way to a one-room clapboard building in the middle of nowhere.

Only thirty miles north of Toronto, and yet a world removed. There were no high-rise condos, no traffic-gridlocked streets in the Marsh. This was farm country, seven thousand acres of rich, organic muck soil, the perfect growing environment for more than sixty crops, everything from romaine and radishes to broccoli, beets, and bok choy.

But Carrie Anne wasn't here for the vegetables, or to admire the endlessly flat landscape of black earth and green fields. She was here to learn how to ride a bike. Needed to master that whole clipless pedal business before her first triathlon in July if she didn't want to look

15

like the complete newbie that she was. Give her a pair of sneakers and she could hold her own in any running event, from a 5K, to a ten-miler, right up to a marathon. Put her in a pool and she could freestyle with the best of them. Admittedly, open water swims were a bit trickier. She had a tendency to go off course; there were no black lines on the bottom of a lake. But she was getting the hang of the art of sighting.

That's how she'd gotten talked into doing a triathlon. A new challenge, her running chums had told her. You can swim and run, they'd said. The bike is the easy part.

Easy for some, perhaps, but Carrie Anne hadn't ridden a bike since grade school, and that one had been a yard sale special. No gears, no shifters on the handlebars. And definitely no clipless pedals.

Even the name was ridiculous. Why call it a clipless pedal if it meant you physically clipped your foot into a cleat? Nonetheless, Carrie Anne Camack wasn't about to be defeated. She didn't accept defeat, not without fighting back, and even if someone did defeat her, she never let it go. Never. She saw the way defeat had eaten away at her mother.

Carrie Anne's motto was "Plan the work and work the plan." So she'd spent the better part of the past winter clipping and unclipping while on the stability of her indoor stationary bike trainer. Now was the time to test it on the roads. Coming to a stop without unclipping in time meant crashing, bike on top of you, while you laid splayed out on the asphalt for all to see, quite possibly in front of a moving vehicle.

It was her boyfriend, Jasper Vanderbilt, an avid cyclist, who'd first recommended the Holland Marsh. Flat roads, mostly local traffic. Lots of other cyclists. He'd grown up in the area; his father still owned a farm there. Carrots and onions, mostly, with a couple of strawberry bushes for the family and a rhubarb plant that grew wilder by the year.

Jasper's face had darkened when he told her about the banker who'd threatened foreclosure against his father and a few of the other farmers in the Marsh, how the merciless pig didn't care to hear about two harsh years of draught and dust storms. Carrie Anne felt the pit of her stomach sour as she remembered the shame her mother had felt when they'd lost their house after the recession hit. The company she'd worked for had declared bankruptcy, which meant not a dime of severance. The loans officer at the bank hadn't given her five minutes to find something else before he pulled the plug. Turned out he was the same guy. Farmers or single moms, it was all in a day's work.

Carrie Anne shook off the memory and concentrated on everything Jasper had told her. Like being mindful of where she was going. There was always the danger of falling into the canal, he warned, seventeen miles of it running alongside the roads, the water flow controlled through a series of pumps. No record of cyclists drowning in the canal, but a few cars had slipped in over the years. Lost control on icy roads in the winter. A couple of drunks in the summer. A few distracted texters. Some of the drivers had made it out alive. Some hadn't.

But this was spring, Carrie Anne was sober, and she refused to think about the possibility of anything going wrong. She pulled the bike out from the back of her rusted-out pickup, set it to rest on the passenger door, and stripped out of her black warm-up pants and matching jacket. Traded her black baseball cap for a bright white helmet. She was already wearing a Canada flag cycling jersey and black spandex shorts that felt as if there was a diaper tucked inside of them. Not exactly a flattering look, but she wasn't here for a beauty contest. She slipped on her bike shoes, staggering a bit on the pavement as the cleats rocked her balance, then put on her gloves, finishing off with a neon yellow vest for added visibility. She took a deep breath, straddled the bike, pushed off and clipped in. So far, so good.

Jasper had suggested a clip/unclip every couple of minutes while riding, with a few stops along the way. Carrie Anne got into a rhythm, gaining confidence as she rode by oversized aluminum-sided storage units and houses shaped like barns with windmill whirligigs spinning out front, all the while taking note of the names of the farm-use only roads: Wilhelmina, Bernhardt, Emma. According to Jasper, Dutch immigrants had originally inhabited the Marsh, though the complexion of the area had diversified significantly over time. Nonetheless, the original settlers had proved to be a hearty breed, recovering from massive flooding thanks to Hurricane Hazel in 1954, and a deadly tornado in 1985, the latter resulting in one road being renamed Tornado Drive. Carrie Anne grinned at the thought. She admired the way the Marshans—if that's what you could call them—thumbed their nose at adversity, the way they refused to be victims.

Clip, unclip, clip, unclip. Carrie Anne clipped back in, turning onto Strawberry Lane and inhaled the pungent smell of celery, onions, and manure, all the while observing the coolie-and-straw-hatted Vietnamese and Mexican workers hunched over in the fields. No one paid her any notice. Cyclists were a common sight in the Marsh, and there was no time to mind anyone else's business.

Maybe if Carrie Anne had stayed focused on the pavement ahead, instead of acting like a tourist on leave from the city, things would have turned out differently. She could have done the fifteen-mile route, carefully mapped out by Jasper, wound her way back to the Asnorveldt Library, and driven home to Toronto, satisfied she'd accomplished everything she'd set out to do. Instead, one minute she was riding along, humming softly, and the next minute she was barreling head on into an enormous wooden crate filled to the brim with freshly picked carrots.

Things could have been worse, she reasoned after the crash, dusting herself off and examining her bike for damage. She could have gone head first into the canal. It wasn't especially deep but it was tinged with a slimy substance that might have been algae or something even guckier. And wet. It was definitely wet.

At least she'd managed to unclip at the very last second. That had to count for something. Carrie Anne was just about to get back on her bike and start cycling when she noticed the hand jutting out of a green garbage bag and the slats in the crate, five well-manicured fingernails pointing towards the sky as if in prayer. She let out a scream that could strip the silk off a corn cob and fainted.

**

It wasn't long before the gawkers arrived, a dozen or so cyclists from a local team, all wearing matching jerseys, a couple of runners, and a leather-skinned man wearing no-name denim jeans and a plaid shirt. One of the runners wetted her brow and then gave her a sip of his water. Some of the cyclists took pictures of the crate and the hand and the fingers with their cell phones, and ghoulishly began to share the news on Twitter, Facebook, and Instagram. None of the coolie- or straw-hatted workers came to see what was going on, though to Carrie Anne's untrained eye, there appeared to be fewer of them out in the field. She texted Jasper and then called the police. Priorities.

Four police officers arrived on the scene and promptly stopped the photo feeding frenzy by inferring that the phones could be confiscated. Sufficiently chastised, the cyclists gave their names and numbers and sped off, followed by the two runners. Carrie Anne was left with the police, the leather-skinned man, and the hand with the manicured fingernails. She turned away and tried not to breathe in the fetid smell of manure wafting from the adjacent field.

It turned out the leather-skinned man owned the crate that held the carrots, although he insisted he had no idea how the hand had gotten in there. "Dumped them in from the flatbed truck this morning, was still a bit dark outside," he said, his face pale beneath his tan. A faint scar over his left eyebrow began to twitch. "Didn't think anyone was in there. Why would I? Never has been before."

Carrie Anne crossed the road and vomited into the canal.

**

The leather-skinned man had a name. Henk Vanderbilt. Jasper's father. The body was a banker known in the area for foreclosing on farm properties, though by all reports, he'd recently approved extending the loan on the Vanderbilt property. Only for a year, mind you, but it removed any motive Vanderbilt might have had for wanting the man dead.

The remaining farmers on the foreclosure list were thoroughly interrogated, and while everyone knew the banker's death was no accident—a dream crusher like that made enemies along the way—no one was charged with his murder or attempt thereof. After a rigorous interview and the insinuation of deportation, three of the farmhands—smokers, they confessed with deep shame, this being Ontario, the "smoke-free" province, after all—admitted to seeing a man dumping a large bag of something into the crate early that morning, certainly well before sunrise. A slender man, they were sure, wearing all black, face hidden by a baseball cap. Of course they assumed it had been carrots. Who would have suspected a man in a garbage bag? A banker from the city, no less.

After a few months and no new leads, the investigation grew cold. As for Carrie Anne, she gave up Jasper, triathlon, and cycling, although not necessarily in that order. When a respectable amount of time had passed she paid a visit to Henk, where she collected a half-dozen strawberry rhubarb pies and a ten-pound bag of onions.

She never ate another carrot.

THE CYCOPATHS

The water in Georgian Bay is chilly, even in the middle of July. In late May, it was downright frosty, but that didn't stop the dozen or so members of the Cycopath Triathlon Team from diving right in. All but one, a finely muscled woman named Cherry, wore long-sleeved neoprene wetsuits. Cherry went sleeveless.

To be fair, Cherry was there that day as our lifeguard, but I suspected her choice had more to do with showing off the new bicycle chain tattoo on her forearm than anything else. Cherry was the founder, president, and enabler of our club, a role she took far too seriously. I just hoped she didn't expect us all to get the same tattoo. I'm not much on commitment, whether it's in the form of relationships, personalized license plates, or body art.

We were at Sunset Point Park in Collingwood, Ontario, a four-season vacation community bordered by the Blue Mountains and the Grey Bruce Peninsula to the south, and Lake Huron's Georgian Bay to the north. Skiing, snowboarding, hiking, fishing, boating, windsurfing, cycling, or swimming, if you were an outdoors enthusiast, Collingwood was your kind of place. But on this unseasonably frigid, gray morning we had the beach to ourselves.

We were there because our team was getting ready for the first triathlon of the season in two weeks time. The purpose of today's exercise was to practice our open water swimming. Cherry had gone out earlier in her kayak and set up a 750-meter course, which she marked with bright orange buoys. They bobbed up and down on the choppy surface like giant pumpkins, a triathlete's trick or treat.

You might think a women's only triathlon club would be kinder and gentler than a mixed or all male group, but you'd be wrong. Get together any group of type-A personalities and there's bound to be some drama, especially if they're in the same five-year age bucket. The Cycopaths were no different, although we usually made the effort to pretend that we were one big, happy family.

At least most of us did. The notable exceptions were the "besties," for whom standing on the podium was a right of passage, and the only place that really counted was first.

Maryanne was by far and away the team's best swimmer, having come up through the ranks as a competitive freelancer, and qualifying for—and winning—Worlds more times than any of us cared to hear about. Katie was our quickest runner, with legs that came up to her ears and a stride to match. Cherry used to say you could crack walnuts on Katie's calves, and she wasn't far off.

When it came to the bike, no one could touch Laura, a deceptively tiny thing that morphed into a machine the minute she straddled the seat and leaned over her aerobars. Laura's motto was "ride it like you stole it," and that pretty much summed up her approach to life: fast, furious, and altogether fearless.

For her part, Maryanne was known to yell "lousy swimmer" when Laura would whiz by her, annihilating the two minutes and twelve seconds Maryanne had gained by getting first out of the water. That might seem unsportsmanlike; in truth, it probably was, but let's face facts. Everyone knows in triathlon, it's the bike that counts. You have to get through the swim. It helps if you're a decent runner, hurts you if you're not. But eight times out of ten, it's the bike that's going to win or lose a race for you.

I'm telling you all of this because if you were to ask me who was most likely to end up getting killed that day, I'd have told you either Cherry or one of the besties.

I would never have picked Sunny, and yet that's exactly who wound up dead.

**

We were back at the beach, changing out of our wetsuits and into dry clothes—all except for Maryanne who was still out there swimming, and Cherry who was watching her from shore—when we realized Sunny was missing. To be honest I can't remember who noticed first. One moment we were chatting, and the next moment we were staring at a lime green bathing cap riding the waves as it drifted further and further off course.

From our vantage point, I couldn't tell if there was a head and body attached to that cap, but the short odds make it likely. The long odds allowed for the possibility that Sunny had taken off her cap, although either way spelled trouble: the main reason you wear a cap in triathlon, beyond keeping your ears warm and dry and being visible in the water, was to have something to wave. That's right. If you found yourself just about ready to drown, you were supposed to have the wherewithal to pull off your cap off and wave it overhead to get someone's attention.

I was still sorting through the possibilities when Cherry hopped in her kayak and began paddling her kayak in the direction of the lime green cap. Laura called 911. The rest of us began the struggle to get back into our wetsuits—a nearly impossible task now that they were indeed wet. But charging into the icy water in our clothes was out of the question, and swimming in our undies meant risking hypothermia, hardly an effective rescue strategy.

Besides, Maryanne was already on the job, alerted by Cherry's shrieks echoing across the water. We stood transfixed as the two of them struggled to lift Sunny's lifeless form over the front of the kayak, watched helplessly as they slowly dragged her body back to shore, Maryanne's right arm wrapped tightly around Sunny's neck, her left hanging on to the side of the boat.

I suppose we all hoped that Sunny would recover once they pulled her onto the beach, but despite Cherry's valiant efforts at CPR, there was no sign of life. It wasn't until Laura finally pulled Cherry off Sunny's unresponsive body that I noticed an angry welt circling her neck like a rattlesnake.

It was beyond belief that Sunny, whose real name was Cordelia, could be dead, let alone strangled in the water. She had been the Miss Congeniality of the Cycopaths, perennially happy, unfailingly supportive, and unlikely to ever beat any of the besties, let alone make it to the podium. In short, everyone loved her.

Or had they? Recently I'd noticed some tension between Sunny and Maryanne. Over the winter, Sunny's 100-meter pool splits had improved into the 1:30s, within sniffing distance of Maryanne. Add drafting into the mix—something that's legal in the open water swim portion of triathlon, although not on the bike—and anything was possible. Sunny could chase down a trail of bubbles like a shark after chum.

And now Sunny was dead, despite Cherry's futile attempts to resuscitate her, and Maryanne had been the last one out of the water. I looked at Maryanne, blue-lipped and shivering, and wondered if staying number one on the swim was enough for her to kill for.

**

I suppose in the spirit of full disclosure I should tell you that I'm one of the team's "wannabes." The antithesis of the besties, the wannabes were never going to podium, not just for lack of natural athletic ability, though that certainly factored in, but because we just didn't have the same bloodthirsty drive for victory. For us, it was enough just to participate in a sport that required you to swim, bike, and run in the same race.

To have fun.

Where the besties would endlessly practice their transitions—the change from swim-to-bike and bike-to-run—all with the goal of shaving off a few precious seconds from their overall finishing time, the wannabes accepted that, for us, mastering the "fourth discipline" was pretty much a waste of time and energy. We didn't spray cooking oil on our bodies to make our wetsuits slip off easier, we didn't care if it took an extra fifteen seconds to slather on some sunscreen before we mounted our bikes on a blistering summer's day, and we weren't about to spend our Friday evenings timing our transitions in Cherry's single car garage.

So it stood to reason, as we stood on the beach silently waiting for the first responders, that we found ourselves divided into two camps: Cherry and the besties on one side and the wannabes on the other. Any camaraderie between us was, at least for the moment, severed, as we stared at each other, assessing the strangers we'd suddenly become. Sunny's body lay a few feet away, her face covered by someone's bubblegum pink beach towel. None of us looked at her.

The fire department and paramedics were quick to arrive, followed closely by the police, who came by boat. There was an initial flurry of activity as they coordinated their efforts, but it was obvious to everyone present that there was no saving this swimmer. I overheard one of the paramedics say they'd have to call the coroner, at which point the firemen dispersed and one of the police officers went back to the boat, presumably to investigate the scene. Her partner, a thickset man with salt and pepper hair, strutted over to where our team had congregated.

"Detective Gilhula," salt and pepper said, introducing himself. "Can someone tell me who the woman was?"

The usually composed Cherry started to sniffle, then broke out into huge gulping sobs. The besties moved closer to her side and made cooing noises. The wannabes averted their eyes and shuffled their feet.

"Cordelia Lemay," I said, realizing no one else was going to volunteer the information. "She was a member of our triathlon team. The Cycopaths. Everyone called her Sunny. Like the sun. Because she was like a ray of sunshine." I realized that I was babbling and stopped talking.

"So she was well liked," Gilhula said.

I didn't know how to answer that. Before today, I would have said yes, but now I wasn't so sure.

"Of course she was well liked," Cherry said, her tears momentarily forgotten. She shot me a venomous glare.

The look wasn't lost on Gilhula, who gave Cherry a tight smile before turning his attention back to me. "You don't seem convinced."

"I thought Sunny was well liked." *At least I did until I spotted the rope marks around her neck.*

"I notice the buoys out there." Gilhula studied us with narrowed eyes. "Which one of you set up the course?"

"I did," Cherry said, her chin tilted high. "We came to Collingwood to practice our open water swims." Her voice took on a defensive snivel. "I received permission from the town. Set everything up properly. I've done it plenty of times before."

If Cherry was looking for absolution, she was looking for it from the wrong man. Gilhula wasn't about to show her—or any of us—any mercy. Not until he'd gotten all the facts.

"Who can tell me what happened?"

Maryanne bit her lip and stared out at the water. The rest of the team looked to Cherry for direction. None was forthcoming. It was as if she'd suddenly disappeared somewhere inside herself. I decided to speak up. If we were ever going to get out of here, one of us would have to.

"It's like Cherry said. We were here practicing our open water swims for our first triathlon of the season. In two weeks. In Milton. The water there is always bone chilling, even with a wetsuit. We thought if we could manage Georgian Bay, we'd be prepared." I shivered at the memory of my face hitting the icy water, the way it had almost left me breathless, thought about Sunny in her lime green cap, floating off course, rope marks on her neck. Had she been left gasping for air, or had her death been swift and merciful? I forced myself to go on.

"The bay was even colder than I expected. I barely managed to swim one round of the course—750 meters—before heading back to the beach. I'm not a particularly fast swimmer. By the time I got back most of the team was already changing into their warm clothes."

"Most of the team," Gilhula said, his eyes flicking from face to face, then back to me.

"Maryanne was still swimming, and Cherry was on shore by her kayak, spotting her. Maryanne's by far the best swimmer on the Cycopaths, and she never seems to be affected by the water temperature." I attempted a smile in her direction, knew it came across as forced. "Then someone, I can't remember who, said 'where's Sunny?' and that's when we noticed her lime green cap floating in the water. It was well off course. I couldn't tell if it was just her cap or . . ." My voice broke. I clenched my fists to keep my hands from trembling, took a deep breath, then another. Hoped someone else would speak up. No one did. Gilhula looked at me expectantly.

"Cherry must have noticed the cap at the same time, or maybe we alerted her, I'm not sure, but all of a sudden she was paddling towards the cap. I've never seen her paddle that fast. The rest of us tried to get back into our wetsuits, but by the time . . . we heard Cherry screaming and Maryanne was already at the kayak. We watched as the two of them pulled Sunny out of the water and brought her back to shore. Laura had already called 911. Cherry tried CPR but it was too late. Sunny was already gone. A couple of minutes later, the paramedics arrived. You know the rest."

Gilhula nodded, his face an impenetrable mask. "Does anyone have anything else to add?"

"I noticed a mark around her neck when I was doing CPR," Cherry said.

"I held Sunny around the neck while Cherry paddled the kayak back to shore," Maryanne said, her face splotched with unattractive blobs of red. "Maybe I held onto her too tightly."

"We'll have to wait for the coroner's office to be certain, but I expect the marks you spotted came from a rope," Gilhula said. "A rope similar to the ones typically used to anchor a buoy. It's unlikely your grip was the cause of death."

"It *can* get pretty intense around the buoys," Maryanne said, the blotches on her face fading slightly. "Everyone kicking and clawing and trying to cut it close so as not to add any unnecessary distance. It's a bit like being inside a washing machine. She must have gone under the surface to avoid the fray, got tangled in the rope somehow."

We all knew Sunny had been practicing diving down and swimming below the surface. But that had been in the pool, where you could see everyone clearly. Cherry had told her more than once it wasn't a safe practice, especially in a lake, that it might even be a disqualifier. Maryanne and Laura had told her too, but Sunny wouldn't listen. She was determined to become a bestie, whatever the cost. She'd even started going to the transition training sessions.

In other words, Sunny was no longer satisfied being a wannabe. How much longer before she'd go after

Katie's running record, or Laura's bike splits? How much longer before she took over as leader of the entire group, replacing Cherry in the role?

And that's when I knew that Cherry, Maryanne, Katie, and Laura were in on it together, not that anyone would ever be able to prove it. Murder on the Orient Express, Cycopath-style. Two people holding her down, one strangling her with the rope. A targeted push by all three to make sure she drifted off course. Cherry standing on shore next to her kayak, waiting until it would be too late.

I looked around at the other wannabes and wondered if any of them had seen anything. If they had, they weren't saying.

Detective Gilhula asked a few more questions, mostly about Sunny's immediate family. It turned out no one really knew anything about her or where she'd come from. He wrote down our contact information. Promised to let us know if there was any resolution to what would almost certainly be ruled an accidental drowning.

We left Collingwood with one less person than when we arrived. Cherry disbanded the Cycopaths a week after the Milton tri—a dismal showing by each and every one of us—and the wannabes found new groups to train with. Laura, Katie, and Maryanne soon found their way back onto the podium, though they now try to avoid entering the same events. To the best of my knowledge, no one ever heard from Detective Gilhula again.

As for me, I gave up triathlon, mostly because I see a lime green swimming cap every time I try to get into the water.

Because I can't help but wonder: what if? What if I'd never told Sunny she had what it took to be the "best" of the besties? What if she'd been satisfied staying a wannabe?

What if?

THE END

About the author

Judy Penz Sheluk's debut mystery, *The Hanged Man's Noose: A Glass Dolphin Mystery*, was published in July 2015 by Barking Rain Press. Her short crime fiction is included in *The Whole She-Bang 2* (Toronto Sisters in Crime, Nov. 2014), *World Enough and Crime* (Carrick Publishing, Nov. 2014), and most recently, *Flash and Bang* (Untreed Reads, Oct. 2015), the first anthology by members of the Short Mystery Fiction Society.

Judy has also contributed to two cookbooks: *Bake, Love, Write: 105 Authors Share Dessert Recipes and Advice on Love and Writing* (Lois Winston, Sept. 2014) and *We'd Rather Be Writing: 88 Authors Share Timesaving Dinner Recipes and Other Tips* (Lois Winston, Oct. 2015).

Judy is a member of Sisters in Crime (International/Toronto/Guppies), Crime Writers of Canada, International Thriller Writers, and the Short Mystery Fiction Society. Find Judy at http://www.judypenzsheluk.com, where she blogs about the writing life and interviews other authors.

Website/Blog: http://www.judypenzsheluk.com

Amazon: amazon.com/author/judypenzsheluk

Facebook: http://www.facebook.com/JudyPenzSheluk

Goodreads:
https://www.goodreads.com/author/show/8602696.Judy_Penz_Sheluk

Pinterest: http://www.pinterest.com/judypenzsheluk

Triberr: http://triberr.com/JudyPenzSheluk

Twitter: @JudyPenzSheluk

www.ingramcontent.com/pod-product-compliance
Lightning Source LLC
Chambersburg PA
CBHW070653130626
46555CB00006B/2851

* 9 7 8 0 9 9 5 0 0 0 7 1 1 *